More of Grandfather's Stories From Germany

Written by Donna Roland
Illustrations by Ron Oden

Adapted from the German Folktale
"Der Heinzelmänchen"

ISBN 0-941996-04-2
Copyright © 1984
OPEN MY WORLD PUBLISHING
1300 Lorna St., El Cajon, CA 92020

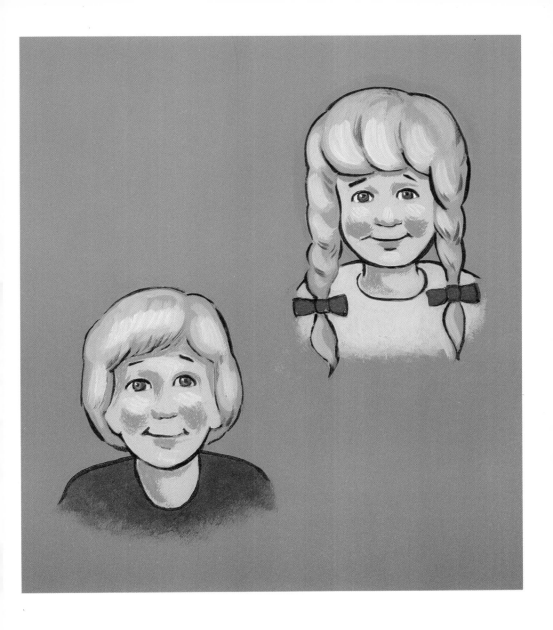

Meet Karl and Hilda.

Karl and Hilda live in America with their mother and father in a little blue and white house.

Karl and Hilda have a grandfather
who lives in Germany, which is far
away across both land and sea.

When Grandfather comes to visit, he tells Karl and Hilda stories they love to hear over and over. The stories he tells them have been told by other German grandfathers for many years.

One of the stories Karl and Hilda love the best is the story about the Mannikins and the green peas. Mannikins are little fairies that live in Germany.

Mannikins are not like most fairies.
They do not live in the woods or in
dark caves. They live inside people's
houses and do lots of work around
the house.

Grandfather has never really seen a
Mannikin, but he has been told
what they look like. Mannikins are
very small, and they wear little
green coats and little green shoes
with big toes.

All day long the Mannikins sleep somewhere in the house. At night, when the people are asleep, the Mannikins come out to play. When they play, they slide down spoons or jump into cups of warm milk that have been left out for them. Mannikins love to play almost as much as they love to work.

No one in all of Germany has more fun than these little men, but when the fun is over, all the work gets done.

Mannikins can be found in many parts of Germany, but long ago most of them lived in the City of Cologne, where the sweet-smelling water comes from. The people of Cologne were always happy, always having fun, and their work was always done.

Every house in Cologne had
Mannikins. The baker would find his
oven clean and full of bread every
day when he got out of bed.

The farmer would find his cows
already milked for him.

Everyone in the City of Cologne was happy. Everyone was liked. But there was one man who was liked the most, and that was the little tailor. The tailor would put out a cup of warm milk and a sweet roll every night for his Mannikins.

The Mannikins liked the little tailor so much that they would put buttons on his coats and lace on the dresses he was making.

When the Mannikins found out that
the little tailor was getting married,
they worked even harder to have
everything just right. The tailor's
house was so clean that it shined.

After their wedding, the little tailor
and his bride lived in the tailor's
house with the Mannikins. His new
bride liked having the work done
by the little men. She always asked
about them, and wanted to see
what they looked like.

She would look all around the house
for them in the day. She would hide
and try to see them when they came
out at night.

She tried and tried to catch them
playing their games or doing their
work, but every night that she would
hide and try to see the Mannikins,
they would not come out.

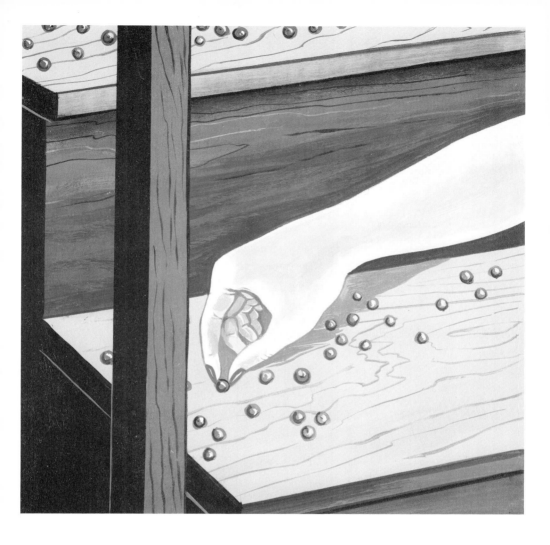

Then one day she came up with a
plan. She would put dried peas up
and down the steps of their house.
She hoped one of the little men
would slip and fall and she would
find him there in the morning. So
that night she put peas on all the
steps like she had planned.

When she got up, she found the green peas where she had left them, but the Mannikins had not come out to play, and no work had been done.

Not one Mannikin could be found.
The buttons had not been put on
the coats, and the lace was on the
table where the tailor had left it.

The Mannikins never came out
again to work or play in the little
tailor's house. Soon all the Mannikins
in the city were gone. Not one
house had Mannikins in it. The
people of Cologne had to get
along without the help of the little
men.

The baker did not find his oven
clean or full of bread when he got
up. The farmer did not find his cows
already milked. And what about the
little tailor?

The tailor's house is very clean. His
coats all have buttons on them and
the dresses he makes all have lots
of lace, not because of the
Mannikins, but because the little
tailor and his bride work very hard.
He is the best tailor he knows how to
be.

Karl and Hilda sometimes wish the
Mannikins would come and live in
their house and help them do their
work. But Grandfather tells them it is
better to do work yourself than to
have it done for you. Just like the
Mannikins and the little tailor,
Grandfather wants Karl and Hilda to
be the best workers they can be.